For my big brother, Art
Love, Dìdi

Henry Holt and Company, *Publishers since 1866*
Henry Holt® is a registered trademark of Macmillan Publishing Group, LLC.
175 Fifth Avenue, New York, NY 10010
mackids.com

Library of Congress Cataloging-in-Publication Data is available.
ISBN 978-1-62779-552-4

Our books may be purchased in bulk for promotional, educational, or business use.
Please contact your local bookseller or the Macmillan Corporate and Premium Sales Department
at (800) 221-7945 ext. 5442 or by e-mail at MacmillanSpecialMarkets@macmillan.com.

First edition—2017 / Designed by Arree Chung and April Ward
The artist used acrylic paint on Rives BFK paper, found paper, and
Adobe Photoshop to make the illustrations for this book.

Printed in China by Toppan Leefung Printing Ltd., Dongguan City, Guangdong Province
1 3 5 7 9 10 8 6 4 2

NINJA CLAUS!

ARREE CHUNG

Henry Holt and Company
NEW YORK

Santa ate my cookies, drank my milk,
and left me this hamster named Ted.

Dear Santa,
Can I have a rat eating
snake this year? I've
been really good exept
that one time. I said
I was sorry!
Love,
Maxwell

This year is going to be **different**.

Dear Santa,

How are you? I am good and thanks for Ted. He eats all the celery I don't want. I've been wondering... are elves taller than kids? Can you read minds? Is your sleigh energy renewable?

This year, I don't want anything. Just stop by for some milk and cookies. And make sure you sit on this

P.S. I hope you can't read minds.

RED CHAIR!

P.P.S. Can I still have a rat eating snake?

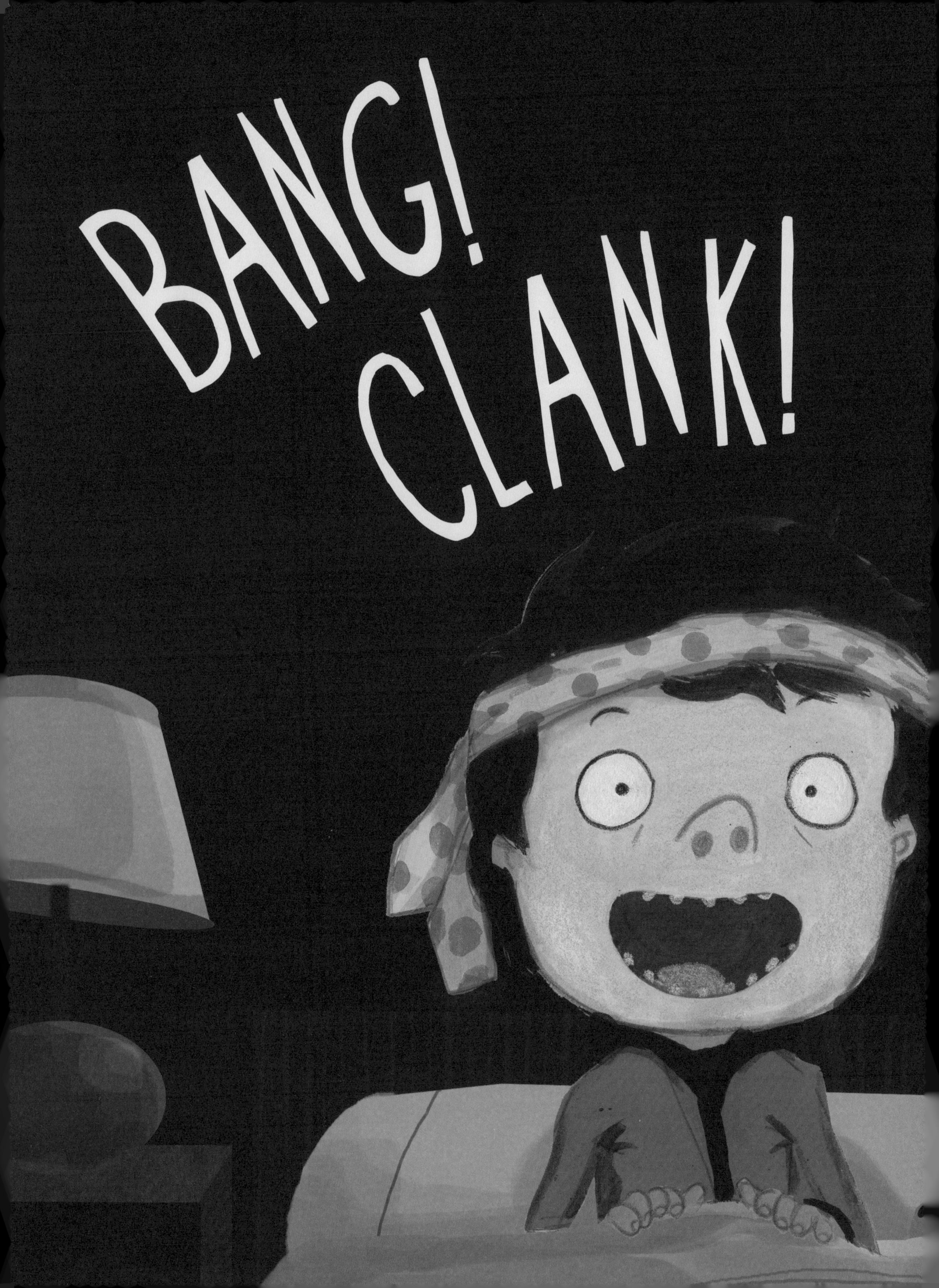
BANG!
CLANK!

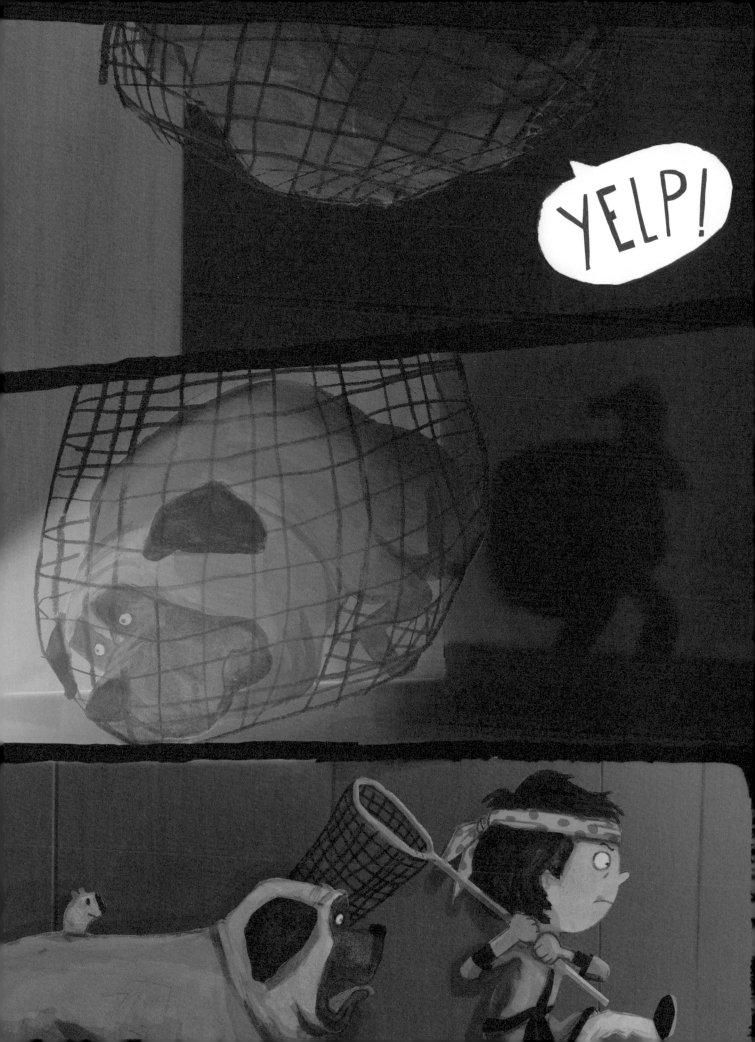

A ninja's traps are impossible to detect.

YIKES!

We caught Santa!

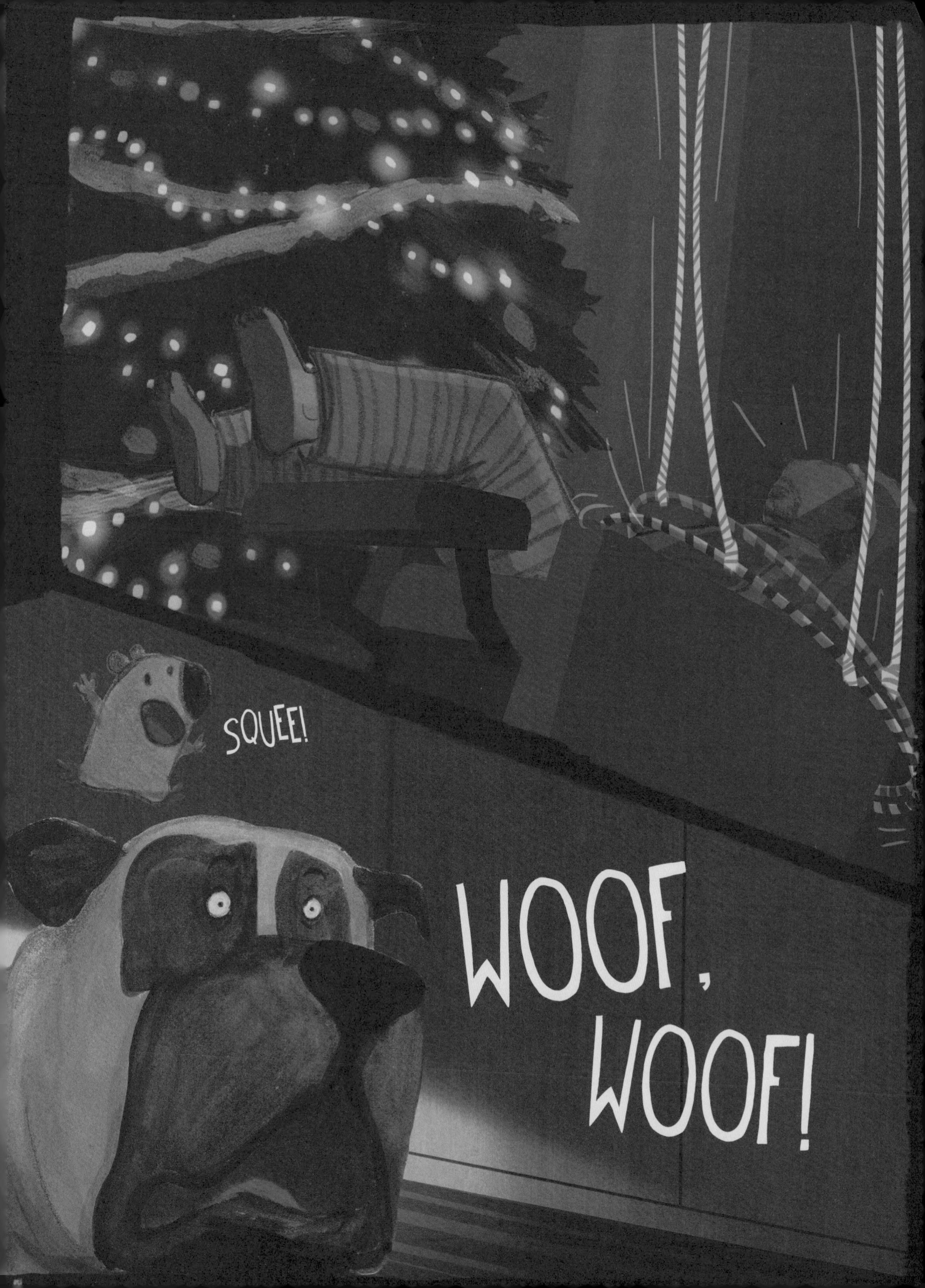
SQUEE!
WOOF,
WOOF!

Those are Santa's cookies!
Wait.
Have you been eating them every year?

Good night, Ted.

Good night, Brutus.

Good night, Maxwell.

The
Ninja Claus
is sneaky,

quick,

clever,

and **kind.**

When his work is done,
the **Ninja Claus**
quietly escapes.

Dear Maxwell,

   Your engineering and ninja skills are very impressive. Do you know how I come and go without being noticed? I wear sneaky Santa shoes made by elves. I had a pair made just for you!

                    Love, Santa

P.S. - Elves are much shorter than kids. My sleigh is fueled by the spirit of Christmas, so yes, it is renewable. I cannot read minds but I can tell if you've been naughty or nice (it's more of a gut feeling).

P.P.S. - No, you can't have a rat-eating snake. He will eat Ted!

Santa is an awesome ninja!

Whew!

Dear Santa,
Thanks for the awesome
ninja shoes. I love them.
Please drop by again
next year.
I'll be waiting
with a big
SURPRISE!